PENELOPE RIGBY Memorial Collection

Presented By THE FRIENDS OF
THE BEVERLY HILLS PUBLIC LIBRARY

# SiMON'S SONG

# SIMON'S SONG

adapted by barbara emberley / woodcuts by ed emberley

prentice-hall, inc., englewood cliffs, n.j.

Printed in the United States of America · J

Simple Simon met a pieman
  Going to the fair;
Said Simple Simon to the pieman,
  "Let me taste your ware."

The pieman said to Simple Simon,
"Show me first your penny."
Said Simple Simon to the pieman,
"Indeed I have not any."

Simple Simon went a-fishing
  For to catch a whale,
But all the water he could find
  Was in his mother's pail.

The wind blew in his collar,
  The rain fell on his head;
Poor Simon never caught a whale,
  He caught a cold instead.

Simple Simon went a-hunting
    For to catch a hare;
He rode a goat about the street,
    But he could not find one there.

He shot an iron weather vane
From off a chicken coop.
"What luck, hoorah! I'll take it home
And make some chicken soup."

Simple Simon went ice-skating,
  On the first of June.
"I like to get here early,
  For the crowds will be here soon."

Simple Simon went to see
  If plums grew on a thistle.
It stung his fingers very much,
  Which made poor Simon whistle.

Sent to fetch the spotted cow,
  He fetched the bull instead.
"This surely is a frisky cow,"
  Was all our Simon said.

When Simon's boat began to sink,
   He did not cry or shout;
He simply drilled another hole,
   To let the water out.

Simple Simon went a-flying
   In a gas balloon.
"I'm going to see my cousin, he's
   The man up in the moon."

"The time has come," our Simon said,
  "To end this silly tune,
And if you see me never, ah!
    You will not see me soon."

Poor Simon, Simple Simon,
    Going to the moon,
And if we see him never, ah!
    We will not see him soon.

**Lyrics:**

1.     Sim - ple Si - mon met a pie - man Go - ing to the fair; ___
2. The pie - man said to Sim - ple Si - mon, "Show me first your pen - ny."
3.     Sim - ple Si - mon went a - fish ing For to catch a whale, ___

Said Sim - ple Si - mon to the pie - man, "Let me taste your ware." ___
Said Sim - ple Si - mon to the pie - man, "'Deed I have not any." ___
But all the wa - ter he could find Was in his moth - er's pail. ___

Poor Si - mon, Sim - ple Si - mon, Show me first your
    Go - ing to the [ fair. ___
          pen - ny.
    For to catch a [ whale. ___

Doo - dum deedle - dum Doodle - dum dee - dum, Doo - dum dyedle - dum
[ dair. ___
[ den - ny.
[ dail. ___

4. The wind blew in his collar,
   The rain fell on his head;
   Poor Simon never caught a whale,
   He caught a cold instead.

   Poor Simon, Simple Simon,
   Caught a cold instead.
   Doo-dum deedle-dum, Doodle-dum dee-dum,
   Doo-dum dyedle-dum dead.

5. Simple Simon went a-hunting
   For to catch a hare;
   He rode a goat about the street,
   But he could not find one there.

   Poor Simon, Simple Simon,
   For to catch a hare.
   Doo-dum deedle-dum, Doodle-dum dee-dum,
   Doo-dum dyedle-dum dare.

6. He shot an iron weather vane
   From off a chicken coop.
   "What luck, hoorah! I'll take it home
   And make some chicken soup."

   Poor Simon, Simple Simon,
   Off a chicken coop.
   Doo-dum deedle-dum, Doodle-dum dee-dum,
   Doo-dum dyedle-dum doop.

7. Simple Simon went ice-skating,
   On the first of June.
   "I like to get here early,
   For the crowds will be here soon."

   Poor Simon, Simple Simon,
   On the first of June.
   Doo-dum deedle-dum, Doodle-dum dee-dum,
   Doo-dum dyedle-dum dune.

8. Simple Simon went to see
   If plums grew on a thistle.
   It stung his fingers very much,
   Which made poor Simon whistle.

   Poor Simon, Simple Simon,
   If plums grew on a thistle.
   Doo-dum deedle-dum, Doodle-dum dee-dum,
   Doo-dum dyedle-dum distle.

9. Sent to fetch the spotted cow,
   He fetched the bull instead.
   "This surely is a frisky cow,"
   Was all our Simon said.

Poor Simon, Simple Simon,
He fetched the bull instead.
Doo-dum deedle-dum, Doodle-dum dee-dum,
Doo-dum dyedle-dum dead.

10. When Simon's boat began to sink,
    He did not cry or shout;
    He simply drilled another hole
    To let the water out.

Poor Simon, Simple Simon
He did not cry or shout.
Doo-dum deedle-dum, Doodle-dum dee-dum,
Doo-dum dyedle-dum dout.

11. Simple Simon went a-flying
    In a gas balloon.
    "I'm going to see my cousin, he's
    The man up in the moon."

Poor Simon, Simple Simon
In a gas balloon.
Doo-dum deedle-dum, Doodle-dum dee-dum,
Doo-dum dyedle-dum doon.

12. "The time has come," our Simon said,
    "To end this silly tune,
    And if you see me never, ah!
    You will not see me soon."

Poor Simon, Simple Simon,
Going to the moon,
And if we see him never, ah!
We will not see him soon.